FERRYBOAT

BY BETSY AND GIULIO MAESTRO

HarperCollinsPublishers

Ferryboat
Text copyright © 1986 by Betsy Maestro
Illustrations copyright © 1986 by Giulio Maestro
Printed in Mexico. All rights reserved.

Library of Congress Cataloging-in-Publication Data
Maestro, Betsy.
  Ferryboat.
  Summary: A family crosses a river on a ferryboat
and observes how the ferry operates.
  [1. Ferries—Fiction]   I. Maestro, Giulio, ill.
II. Title.
PZ7.M267Fe   1986   [E]   85-47887
ISBN 0-690-04519-0
ISBN 0-690-04520-4 (lib. bdg.)

Designed by Trish Parcell
10 9 8 7 6 5

If you want to cross the river at Chester,
you have to take the ferry.

All day long, the ferry goes back and forth,
taking cars and trucks and people across the river.
Toot! Toot! Here it comes!

The Captain steers the ferry into the slip.
It stops and the gates go up.
The cars and trucks drive off.

Now it's our turn.
The ferryman says, "Drive on up."
We pull in behind a big van.
It's a tight squeeze!

If you don't have a car, you can still ride the ferry.
Some passengers walk up the ramp to board.
The gates close. Full load!

The Captain turns on the engine and we're all set to go.
The ferry doesn't have to turn around.
Its front is the same as its back!

The ferryman gives us our ticket.
Now, we can get out of our car to see the river.
There's so much to look at.
Boats are everywhere.
And there's a duck family paddling by!

The big engine vibrates and hums.
We can feel the ferry moving under our feet.

The water spray wets us a little.
Our damp faces feel cool in the wind.

There's the Captain sitting up high in the wheelhouse.
He is busy watching out for other boats.
Here comes a big riverboat.

We're coming to the other side.
The Captain toots the whistle.
Everyone hurries back to their cars.
Slowly, the ferry glides into the slip.
Steer carefully! There's not much room
between the pilings.

We're stopping now.
The ferryman works the pulleys
to lower the ramp.
The gates go up and we can drive off.

One by one, the cars and trucks come off the ferry and drive away. We'll stay and watch while the ferry loads up for another crossing.

We'll go back tonight on the last ferry run
of the day. If we miss it, we'll have to drive
way up the river to the bridge.

And in the spring, the ferry will be ready
for another busy year on the river.
Toot! Toot!

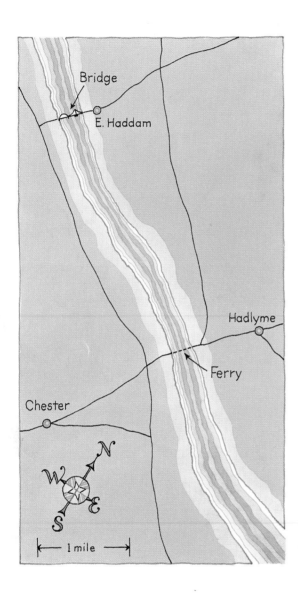

HISTORICAL NOTE

The Chester-Hadlyme Ferry began operation in 1769. It was then called Warner's Ferry, because it was owned and operated by Jonathan Warner (1728–1810) who owned the land on both sides of the Connecticut River. The ferry connected King's Highway in Fort Hill, Parish of Chester in Saybrook (Connecticut), to the Norwich Road in Lyme across the river. Today, the road is called Route 148 and the ferry connects the towns of Chester and Hadlyme.

The first ferry was a barge with a towboat propelled by sail or long poles. During the years of the Revolutionary War, the ferry was used to transport supplies. In 1879, a steam-powered barge replaced the older type of ferry. In 1882, the ferry became known as the Chester-Hadlyme Ferry, the name it still has. The ferry was operated by the town of Chester from 1877 until 1917, when it was turned over to the State of Connecticut, to be run by the Department of Transportation.

The Chester-Hadlyme Ferry is the second oldest ferry service in continuous use in Connecticut. The oldest is the Rocky Hill Ferry, which is also the oldest in the United States.

The 65-foot Selden III began service in the spring of 1950.